Pony Express Christmas

Pony Express
CHRISTMAS

SIGMUND
BROUWER

Tyndale House Publishers, Inc.
Wheaton, Illinois

Stopping briefly at way stations every ten to fifteen miles for a fresh horse, Pony Express riders covered about seventy-five miles each in a relay system, which stretched two thousand miles from St. Joseph, Missouri to Sacramento, California. With 190 way stations, the route took riders through Nebraska, Wyoming, and Nevada. Winter did not stop the Pony Express, and logistically it was a very successful way to move mail across the frontier—for five dollars an ounce, the delivery time of ten days was half of its competitor's, the Overland Mail Company, which used a longer route through the Southwest. While blizzards were unsuccessful in shutting down the Pony Express, financial losses and the completion of overland telegraph connections brought the freighting company to an end with bankruptcy in October 1861, only eighteen months after it began.

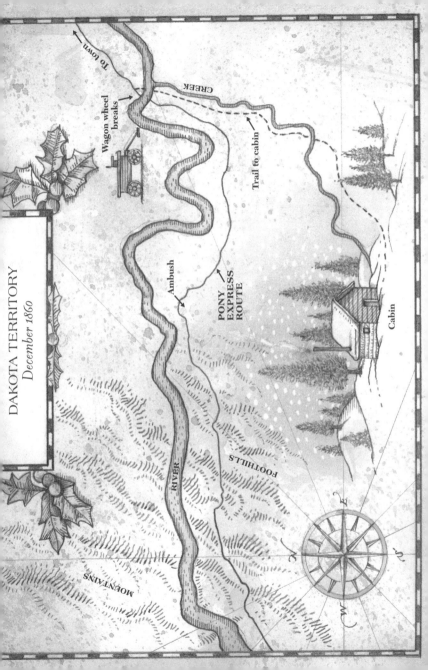

Visit Tyndale's exciting Web site at www.tyndale.com

Visit Sigmund Brouwer's exciting Web site at www.coolreading.com

Edited by Curtis H. C. Lundgren

Designed by Catherine Bergstrom

Scripture quotations are taken from the *Holy Bible,* New Living Translation, copyright © 1996. Used by permission of Tyndale House Publishers, Inc., Wheaton, Illinois 60189. All rights reserved.

Library of Congress Cataloging-in-Publication Data

Brouwer, Sigmund, date
    Pony express Christmas / Sigmund Brouwer.
      p. cm.
    Summary: A Pony Express rider stops to help a family in need at Christmas despite his mission to deliver the mail without delay.
    ISBN 0-8423-4018-1
    [1. Pony express—Fiction. 2. Christmas—Fiction. 3. Robbers and outlaws—Fiction. 4. Frontier and pioneer life—West (U.S.)—Fiction. 5. West (U.S.)—Fiction. 6. Christian life—Fiction.] I. Title

PZ7.B79984 Po 2000
[Fic]—dc21   00-034343

Printed in the United States of America

05	04	03	02	01	00			
9	8	7	6	5	4	3	2	1

PROLOGUE

Above the valley

no hawk drifted in the cold eastern wind in search of prey that December afternoon, for its efforts would have been in vain; ground squirrels slumbered deep in burrows, pressed each against the other for warmth; and jackrabbits huddled beneath thorny brush, ears tucked back in their thick fur to retain heat. All of the animals— from bedded-down deer to blue jays tucked among the branches of conifers to coyotes desperately scratching in the tall brown grass for mice—were served well by the instinct given them by God and knew a storm approached.

Had there been a hawk in the wind, however, its view would have encompassed in the distance the jagged snow-topped granite of the range of mountains that splintered the Territory from this southern border all the way to the north. A river followed pine-dotted foothills down from those majestic mountains to this grassland valley, where water that had so recently tumbled over icy boulders began to freeze as it slowed and flattened between willow-lined banks before spilling onto the plains farther east.

Great clouds of purple and gray rose in a huge blossom behind the jagged horizon. In height and width, the great clouds began to dwarf the mountains. These clouds were sustained by a growing wind, which threw bitter granules of snow that rose and fell with the gusts that grasped at the land miles and miles ahead of the storm. Here in the valley, this hard snow gave warning as it rattled bushes and grass and long-dead flowers that had once stretched so lovely and vibrant toward the peaceful suns of spring and summer days.

With its keen eyes—had it been foolish enough to ride the winds that cold December afternoon—this hawk would most certainly have seen a drama about to unfold hundreds of feet below.

At the western end of the valley, where eons of water had cut through low granite cliffs, the river first entered from the foothills. Because this was the most gradual slope, a wagon trail hugged the banks. This was the only route to and from a distant mountain pass.

Two men crouched among the clefts of the granite. Although plainly visible from above—figures almost black in greasy long coats and battered hats—these men were well hidden from any who might travel out of this desolate valley. Indeed, farther up toward the foothills, away from where the cliffs squeezed the wagon trail into a shadowed gap, two stolen saddled army horses were tethered to a scrawny tree, ready for the return of these men.

A hawk, of course, would not recognize the long thin objects cradled by these hidden men as rifles, nor would the hawk appreciate the deadliness and accuracy of those Winchester .44s. A hawk, then, would not have had any sense of foreboding had it been there, high above the valley in the storm's wind.

For there was a third man in the valley.

He rode a big roan horse at full gallop along the wagon trail, heading directly toward those armed men who guarded the narrow gap between the cliffs.

*   ✻   *

East and south of that desolate valley where two gunmen awaited a lone rider, nestled among hills that seemed to tremble in the fall with the whispering, shaking sunburnt leaves of hundreds of aspen saplings, there was a small log cabin built near a spring.

The grass around the cabin had long since been trampled by the activities of children and horses and wagon wheels, so that the path that led to the spring from the cabin was a narrow rutted groove, slightly deeper than the dirt and rock on each side.

A half-finished corral stood behind the cabin on one side, and on the other, an outhouse that leaned in one direction, although the wood used in its construction was store bought and still green.

Against the north wall of the cabin, as added protection against the snow that would soon arrive, split logs had been stacked almost to the eaves of the roof. As proof of the reason for the logs, smoke rose from the chimney, to be snatched away immediately by the wind.

Inside, a tired woman with three young children tried to keep busy with any activity that might take her thoughts away from the worry that swelled in her chest and shortened her breath the longer they were alone.

*   ✽   *

One full day of travel east and north of this cabin with the woman and three boys, a collection of unpainted wooden buildings formed a small town where the river from the valley joined a larger river. It was the town closest to the mountains, one of the few towns in the Territory, the only civilization for hundreds upon hundreds of square miles in any direction.

The roads to the town were merely wagon trails. The road that led west to the mountain pass from this town was the wagon trail that cut through the valley where two armed men waited in ambush for the third.

This road split at a creek a few miles before that valley. From this divide, the main wagon trail continued toward the mountain pass; it was on this trail, a few miles from that spot, that the rider in full gallop proceeded toward cliff gaps.

The other trail at that point was a smaller, less used trail, which meandered ten miles south to isolated ranch houses. One of those houses was the cabin among the hills where a woman anxiously waited with her three young children.

And at the split of the two trails, a man and a boy sat on an open wagon—horseless and with a broken axle—stuck squarely on the far bank of the creek. The man lost in his thoughts, staring down at the splint on his right leg. The boy bewildered by the despondency of his father. Neither wanted to talk, both afraid it might bring them to the last words they'd heard before leaving the cabin, the woman, and the three other children.

The first granules of snow from the approaching storm hit them squarely in their faces.

Unlike the animals of the surrounding wilderness, this man had not had any awareness of the weather ahead. Other travelers, much wiser, had looked at the sky and decided against the risk.

As the wind-driven snow raked across their exposed faces, the man bowed his head in prayer. It was all that he had left, this hope and trust.

1

At five hundred yards away

the drumming of a horse's hooves on frozen ground reached the two who waited in ambush. At four hundred yards, the horseman broke into view, still at full gallop.

The rising clouds to the west had covered the weak December sun, giving the valley a uniform gray. The traveler and horse stood out clearly in contrast.

Neither of the men in ambush moved.

"That him?" The younger, smaller man coughed. "The Pony Express rider?"

"No," his older brother said. "That's a schoolmarm."

"I was just asking."

"And I'm telling you I planned this good. He comes through like clockwork, which is why we're here. So don't ask dumb questions."

The horse continued closer.

"Steady now," the older brother said. He called himself Kentucky and never gave anyone his last name. Nor did he ever remove his hat, except to sleep. He was a large man and, despite missing several of his bottom front teeth, was vain enough about his appearance to hate the fact he was bald except for the long fringes of hair that hung below his hat. "With the fever you got, you're shaking so bad we best wait 'til he's close enough we can see his eyes."

"If you told me that once, you told me that a hundred times already." Reb, the other man, shivered. Reb figured if his older brother was able to give himself a name like Kentucky, he too could change his own name, Wilbur, to something more stylish. Reb was ten years younger and did the best he could to look older by growing a scraggly beard, which on occasion he'd been forced to shampoo with lye soap to rid his face of fleas. "Next you're gonna say he'll come through here so fast we're only gonna get one shot, maybe two."

"Glad to find out you've been heeding my words,"

Kentucky answered. "Now shut your yap and get ready."

Both men had earlier propped their rifles on the boulders that hid them. This had made the waiting easier and ensured steadier aim.

Their prey was now two hundred and fifty yards away.

Each eased back the hammer of his rifle.

Kentucky drew a breath and held it, looking down the barrel of his rifle with both eyes open, for that was his manner of preparing to shoot. Reb squinted his left eye shut and peered through his sights with his right eye. Despite their mannerisms, neither could shoot well.

Now the rider was two hundred yards away, the incline of the slope hardly slowing the horse.

"Easy now," Kentucky whispered, as if they were hunting deer. "Don't spook him."

A thick gust of snow briefly obscured the vision of the shooters.

When the snow passed a second later, they saw that the man had slowed to a trot. He was still one hundred and seventy-five yards away, clear in their sights so that they could see that his buckskin gloves were new enough to be an undirtied yellow.

"What now?" Reb whispered back, his teeth clicking because of the cold and because of the fever that gripped him. "Surely, he don't see us."

"Long as he's still coming," Kentucky grunted, "it only helps us that he's dropped his pace."

The horse now slowed, approaching the incline with a halting gait. It was still one hundred and fifty yards away from the gap between the cliffs.

Wind from the gap drove away the sound of the horse's heavy gasps for air as its sides heaved, but the shooters saw the vapor from the horse's lungs as it froze in the air.

"He's the Pony Express man sure enough," Reb said, his voice almost inaudible. He shook violently, and it took him effort to stay crouched behind his rifle. "They ain't supposed to slow up for nothing. It ain't right, him taking the horse out of a gallop. He sees us. I know he sees us. Let's shoot now."

A thicker gust of wind careened through the canyon gap, bringing another sheet of snow that blocked their vision.

When the rider reappeared from the swirling snow, he and his horse were at a standstill. The horse pranced back and forth, as if the man could not decide to move ahead or backward.

"He don't see us," Kentucky answered with equal quiet. "Otherwise, he'd be staring up here at the rocks instead of looking back over his shoulder."

The smaller man had no reply to this.

The Pony Express man *was* looking backward into the dim gray of the valley.

"Maybe he's thinking of going back," Kentucky said. "Now's the time. But make it count. We miss him or wing him, we won't get a chance like this again."

Yet a third blast of snow covered them.

Only for a moment.

It was as if that third blast of snow had been enough to drive away the man and his horse. In the next second, the Pony Express man was at full gallop again, in the opposite direction.

Reb remained bent over his rifle. He was about to squeeze the trigger on his disappearing target when Kentucky pulled him off the rifle.

"Don't waste the shot," Kentucky hissed. "We don't have bullets to spare. Last thing we want to do is give him warning."

Reb straightened and coughed for a long spell and finally spit. It was a weak effort and rolled down his chin and onto his coat, showing blood. He slapped his hands together. His gloves were worn and gave little protection against the cold. "Well, I ain't gonna wait here for him to come back. In this wind, it'll kill me, I promise you. What are we gonna do?"

"I know it wasn't us that turned him around," the first man said. "So we're gonna follow and see what did."

2

the three small boys in the cabin shared a corn-shuck mattress in the corner farthest from the door. They sat on the mattress now, backs to the wall, with a thick blanket over their legs.

The interior of the cabin was warm. For all that the family lacked, one of the items was not firewood. The black stove in the middle glowed with heat, and a pot of water rested on top of the stove to throw humidity into the air.

Their ma knelt in front of a small fir tree. She had spent the afternoon cracking walnuts, then running a thread through the centers of the nut meats with a needle. When she had finished, she had a long string that she now draped over the branches of the tree.

"Looks purty, Ma," the middle boy said. Six years old, his name was Seth. He'd lost his front teeth in the previous couple of weeks, and as a result, had acquired a charming lisp that usually brought a smile to his ma's face.

Except for now. She was doing all she could to hide her fear.

"It does at that," she said, not realizing how tight-lipped and stern she appeared. Grace Sparling was a young woman, not even into her thirties, but at this moment she felt ancient.

If she allowed herself to think about it, she would have admitted that it was not only in this moment that she felt ancient. For months, with growing frequency and in all sorts of unguarded moments, the phrase "godforsaken wilderness" had popped into her mind. Each time it happened, she forced the thought away, telling herself that a good wife and a good Christian did not complain. But did a good wife and a good Christian deserve the dirt that seeped through the cracks of the cabin and the mosquitoes that attacked all through the summer and the constant worry about a bear or cougar taking away one of her children?

And now this—the fear that her husband and oldest son might not return. Ever.

She had begun to feel old and bitter, and this sense alone added to her bitterness. She'd stopped looking in the cracked hand-held mirror because her black hair had started to show a few strands of gray, and wrinkles had begun to form at the edges of her eyes and mouth. She didn't even have much for clothing to make her feel feminine, and now, as always, wore a faded dress, and to keep warm in the cabin, kept on a shirt of her husband's, which flapped around her waist.

"Ma, looks purty." Caleb, the youngest, had just learned to talk and constantly echoed his brothers. "Looks real purty."

Not even Caleb's sweet voice brought her any joy in this moment. She stepped back from the tree and shook her head at it, worry lines creasing her forehead.

The tree was decorated with bits of colored rag that

she'd torn from one of her two good dresses. The walnuts she'd been holding on to since the summer, keeping them hidden in a box behind the bed in the upstairs loft. In October, she'd managed to buy some hard-rock candy, and she would surprise the boys with that in the morning. Other than that, the Christmas season had promised little cheer.

Now it was getting dark. A storm was about to hit. And Jeremiah, her busted-up husband, and her oldest boy, Noah, were somewhere out on the trail.

She couldn't help imagining all the worst.

They'd run into Indian trouble, perhaps. She'd been told there had been no uprisings in the five years since the army cleaned up this portion of the Territory, but what if a couple of warriors had drifted back and found her husband and boy all alone on the trail?

What about bears? In the fall, she'd walked into a clearing and startled a big black bear, which had run away instead of toward her, but she fell asleep nightly with visions of what that beast might have done to one of her boys. It was not much consolation when Grace remembered that bears hibernated; she hadn't lived here long enough to fully know the habits of bears and was able to convince herself that they might venture out at any time.

What if . . .

Grace forced herself to block out any further thoughts. She found a candle and lit it. Although it wasn't yet evening, the sky had darkened so much that the two meager glass windows didn't bring in much light.

Grace set one candle on the ledge of the window. Those panes of glass had cost dearly, more than they could afford. Perhaps tonight, she thought, the light of the candle through the window would bring her husband and boy home and justify what they had spent for the luxury of glass windows.

". . . sounded like maybe wolves," she heard Josiah saying, the word *wolves* taking her out of her thoughts. "They grow big out in these parts. I heard the size of horses, with teeth like butcher knives and—"

"That's enough," she snapped, turning back to the bed.

She marched toward her eight-year-old and grabbed his ear between her thumb and forefinger. "You and I both know that noise is the wind. And you have no right trying to scare your two younger brothers!"

She dropped her grip on his ear and raised her hand to slap his head.

Grace caught the frightened look on Josiah's face and realized in that moment that her fierceness had startled him badly. She also realized that she wasn't angry at Josiah but at her husband. And at God. Just two years ago, they had lived in a comfortable house in Chicago. Now they had no money left and might not even make it through the winter. All because Jeremiah had some romantic notion about letting his boys grow up in the Wild West and giving the family a chance to build up a ranch that would someday be worth a hundred times more than he could save in a lifetime of school teaching. But this dream was ashes.

Neither Jeremiah nor God had done much providing lately.

Still, Grace had no right to take out her frustration and anger and sense of helplessness on her boys.

She hugged Josiah, mortified at how close she had come to striking her own child in anger for the first time.

Added to her growing guilt was her memory of her recent farewell. Only it had not been a farewell but a venting of the same bitterness and anger that filled her now. If only she hadn't had words with her husband. He was a fool to go to town, but she should have hidden her doubt. Especially with all that had happened to them lately.

Fool.

The word echoed in her mind.

Fool. Her last word to him had been *fool*. She had told him he was a hopeless dreamer, not much more than a fool, unable to provide properly for his family, and that he was especially a fool for leaving his family to go into town. Then she'd angrily repeated the word *fool* one final time for emphasis. With their oldest boy, Noah, listening to all of it.

How could she have done that? Torn down her husband in front of the boy? It broke her heart now to think of the sad pain on her husband's face as he turned away from her to go to the horse and wagon.

What if she never had the chance to speak to him again? What if . . .

"I am so sorry," she murmured to Josiah. She would keep her mind off the past and give what she could to the boys with her now. She smoothed Josiah's hair with one hand as she continued to hold him tight with her other. "So sorry. You don't deserve that. Just promise me you won't scare your brothers with more stories. Not now, all right?"

Her tears, however, frightened the three boys more than her anger. Until now, she'd always managed to hide her frustration and sadness, choosing times when she was alone to let the tears flow.

They'd never seen her cry before.

3

Grady O'Neill swung off his horse
at the top of the bank. He surveyed the man still sitting
on the horseless wagon with the broken axle. He was
looking in the opposite direction, not even aware of his
return. The boy was off to the side looking for wood.

Greenhorn, he thought about the man; *he isn't even
making a move to get ready for the night. What does he
expect, an angel?*

If so, he added to himself, *the greenhorn is definitely
in for disappointment.* Grady had been called plenty of
things, but angel was not one of them.

He led his horse down toward the wagon, glad for
the scarf that covered his face from the intense cold.
The temperature had dropped considerably in the last
half hour since Grady had first seen the wagon.

Earlier, Grady had broken over the hill that led down to the creek. He'd seen the wagon without a horse and the man and the boy and told himself to keep his horse at full gallop. With the snowstorm ahead, night approaching, and twelve miles to go to the next way station, he couldn't afford to stop.

No Pony Express rider could. Not if he wanted to keep his job. Pony Express riders had simple and strict instructions: Deliver the mail at any cost. Grady knew just stopping his horse could get him fired.

The settler, of course, had waved his hat as Grady thundered down the slope. Waved it valiantly as Grady swerved on entering the creek to go past the wagon. Grady hadn't even lifted his hands from the reins to wave back. Riding at full gallop took concentration and perfect balance.

"Hey, mister!" the man had shouted as soon as he began to understand that Grady meant to keep riding. "Hey, mister! I need help!"

Not from me, Grady had told himself, shutting his ears against the man's voice. But Grady had made the mistake of looking over as his horse slowed to step across the rocks on the up slope on the other side of the creek. Grady caught sight of the man's face, the slump of his shoulders, like he'd just lost all hope because Grady was passing him by.

Grady had pulled back on the reins.

Just one minute, he'd told himself. He'd stop long enough to explain why he couldn't help. This settler would understand. Everyone had heard of the Pony Express and how the riders were able to deliver a letter from California to Missouri in an unbelievable ten days.

"Sorry, not much I can do," Grady had said, pointing at the mailbags on his saddle. "I ride for the Express. They're expecting me ahead. When I get there, I'll send someone back."

Grady had galloped onward, pushing up the creek bank and following the wagon trail. Greenhorn or not, the man would know of the Pony Express station at the Weyburn ranch. So it wasn't like he was leaving the man and the boy stranded without any hope of rescue.

But within a couple of miles, Grady had known there

would be no rescue this night. Not when he'd broken into the openness of the next valley and seen how big the storm clouds were against the horizon of the mountains. Grady guessed that in less than two hours, a man would be traveling blind with all the snow that would hit. Even if someone from the Weyburn ranch wanted to help out, it would be impossible. Nor was it likely, given the storm, that anyone else would pass by the man and boy.

Grady had kept riding though, telling himself the man and boy would take care of themselves. Surely they had supplies and common sense. Besides, Grady had kept arguing with himself, if he turned back, he'd never make the Weyburn ranch. It would cost him his job if he failed to show up with the mail, because another rider was waiting to take it farther west. If he lost his job, how would he be able to continue to court Lucy Weyburn?

Yet, much as he argued with himself, Grady had not been able to shake the image of the man's slumped shoulders. Finally, fifteen minutes after leaving them, when the first real blast of snow had hit Grady, he'd reluctantly given in to what he'd known from the beginning he must do. A man just didn't leave behind someone who needed help.

He'd turned around just before reaching the pass and headed back to the man and the boy.

Why did he have to be the one, Grady had griped again and again while galloping back to the creek. Why not anyone else who might have ridden past the stranded man and boy?

Grady shook his head one final time before yelling hello downward to the wagon.

Shoot, by now he could have already been five miles closer to Lucy Weyburn and her wonderful perfume and dazzling smile. And he'd still have a job.

He kicked a rock as he led his horse to the wagon.

This wasn't going to be much of a Christmas, he grumbled in the silence of his mind. What rotten luck that he'd been forced to turn back.

4

Swirling snow

covered Kentucky and Reb on their horses as they slowly rode side by side on the wagon trail, away from the mountains and out of the valley.

It had taken them five minutes to retrieve their horses and begin pursuit. Their rifles were riding on top of the saddlebags, which held precious little else. They were low on ammunition and had no more food or whiskey. Aside from blankets rolled and strapped behind their saddles, they were traveling as light as possible, not by choice.

With the storm gaining force, however, they dared not chase the Pony Express rider at a gallop, much less a trot. Visibility had lessened to the point where the hills that outlined the valley had long been lost in the gray horizon, and at best they could only see thirty or forty feet ahead. Last thing either man wanted was a horse to step in a hole and break a leg.

The only mercy was the fact that the wind was at their backs. The driven snow collected on their shoulders and rear brims of their hats.

"What say we stop and build a fire," Reb yelled above the wind. His shivering was almost unbearable. "There will be another time for this."

"Fire don't do much good when a man's belly is tight with hunger," Kentucky yelled back. "This snow will slow him down too, and maybe we'll find him at his own fire. Once we get that Pony Express mailbag, then our problems are over."

"We'll have the law after us again," Reb shouted. The effort it took dizzied him, and the edges of his vision blurred with darkness. He just wanted to crawl under his blanket and let the snow cover him. "I just don't know that I'll be much good in the saddle. This fever—"

"Quit your whining!" Kentucky shouted back. "You

been using that fever as an excuse for a week now, and I'm sick of you being sick! Hear me?"

Like I been hearing you since we were boys, Reb thought. But he didn't say it, just kept it inside like he always did.

They rode on, with Reb trying to remember if ever he had made a suggestion that Kentucky agreed to. And now that Reb thought of it, he realized this life had been Kentucky's decision, prompted by dreams of easy money and little work. Well, Reb thought, it had turned out just the opposite. They were on stolen horses and empty stomachs, and it had been that way for so long that some mornings Reb could hardly climb onto his saddle.

Reb didn't know that he could take this life much longer. He'd been dreaming lately about three square meals a day and a small but steady salary, even if it meant backbreaking work and listening to Kentucky go on and on how only fools made themselves slaves to a trail boss. Thing was, a man with folding money might even be able to court a lady.

He wondered if he should bring that up with Kentucky but was having a difficult time finding the energy to say much more. So he concentrated on staying straight in his saddle. The darkness closed in on the edges of his vision again. Reb's stomach clenched in agony, and he shivered harder, even as sweat pushed through the skin of his forehead and froze on his face.

Kentucky and Reb continued east, pushed by the wind.

It didn't take long for snow to cake the hind ends of the horses. They began to falter. These animals had been pushed hard over the last month, and neither Kentucky nor Reb made it a habit to be overly concerned about the welfare of their horseflesh.

"Just a few miles more!" Kentucky finally shouted. His own hands and face had become numb. "If we don't find him by then, we'll look for shelter. A warm fire and a tight belly are better than freezing to death!"

Reb didn't reply.

Kentucky hadn't noticed earlier, for he'd kept his head down as they plodded.

Reb had fallen forward in his saddle, to clutch the neck of his horse.

As Kentucky looked over to see why Reb hadn't jumped at his new suggestion, Reb slid out of his saddle and hit the ground between the two horses.

5

"Ma," Josiah said.

"Tell us how you and Pa met."

Grace looked over from the stove. She'd decided to keep herself busy by making biscuits with the last of the flour.

Josiah had an earnest expression on his face. She well recognized it. It was almost identical to the look that often crossed her husband's face.

"You've heard me tell you that story a hundred times," she said, suppressing a smile. She knew why Josiah was asking. He was only eight years old but, like his father, had a sensitive side that he could not keep hidden from the harshness of the world. Josiah, even at his young age, was fully aware of his mother's troubled sadness and furthermore understood how much it cheered her to tell this familiar story.

"Tell us, tell us," Seth said. It came out like "telluth, telluth," and Grace finally did smile.

Caleb clapped his pudgy little hands. "Tell us. Tell us."

Grace knew she should fall down on her knees and thank God right then and there for how much she loved these boys. But God was so far away from her, and she felt all her prayers to him had been hollow words directed into the uncaring wilderness. Another thought occurred to her. It had been two weeks since she'd prayed quietly herself. Sure, she'd prayed aloud with the boys as she put them to sleep each night, but that was part of her duty.

"Tell us! Tell us!" the boys shouted.

With a wooden spoon, she slapped out the biscuit dough into dollops and put them into the stove. The stove was a Franklin, their last purchase with the inheritance that they'd brought into the West, and every day she was grateful for that stove.

Grace wiped her hands on her apron, removed it, and walked over to the corn-shuck mattress in the corner, from where the three boys had been watching her with large, grave eyes.

She sat beside them, and they crowded around her.

"It was at a church social," she said. "I was minding my own business, talking to some of my friends, and I heard the biggest commotion you could imagine. Some young man on the other side of the hall had just told a story, and everyone around him was laughing like there was no tomorrow. Naturally, my friends and I were curious. But being the ladies we were, we didn't dare intrude."

"Tell us the story he told, Ma," Caleb urged. "We love to hear about that."

Indeed they did. For all his shortcomings as a rancher and settler, their father had an amazing gift as a storyteller. Grace's renditions, at best, were second rate, but it was still enough to captivate the boys, who never minded hearing her repeat stories that they had already heard a dozen times from their father.

Grace's best memories of the cabin—and there weren't many—were of the nights when all of them sat inside, with a candle or two burning, and her husband leaning forward in the shadows to bestow upon them another whopper. Those were the times when she was able to forget all their troubles.

Only now, those same memories flooded her as she began to retell the old story. Sadness infused her voice, for it only reminded her that already it was near dark, and there was no sign of Jeremiah or her oldest boy.

What kind of Christmas, she wondered, was this going to be?

6

"Mister," the man said, "you're an answer to prayer."

Grady snorted. "Then the Lord has a sense of humor I'll never understand. My own prayers involved other matters."

Grady had walked his horse up to the wagon and introduced himself to the man and boy.

He discovered the man's name was Jeremiah Sparling. He wore a chewed-up floppy hat. His dark beard covered most of his face. His clothes were worn and ragged. The boy beside him, Noah, seemed large for the jacket and pants stretched short and tight.

"I'm sorry for that," Jeremiah said. "Truly sorry. If my leg wasn't busted up like this . . ."

Grady regretted his sour attempt at humor. He was

in this too far to back out, and since it had to be done, he might as well be gracious about it.

"Bad luck, huh?" Grady said, surveying the wagon.

"You don't know the half of it," the man said. He described what had happened. While crossing the creek, the horse had broken through a skiff of ice and slipped on muddy rocks. The ice had cut the horse's hock as it stumbled. In panic, the horse had tried to bolt.

Because the man was unable to stand and balance without his crutches, he had mishandled the reins from his awkward sitting position on the bench of the wagon. The rear axle of the wagon had slammed into a rock as one of the back wheels fell through the ice into a hole hidden by the water. The horse's momentum had taken the wagon out of the creek and onto land, but no farther.

On the other side of the creek, the wagon had stopped dead among large rocks. The axle had snapped with the sickening sound of a breaking thighbone. The horse had reared in more panic, tangling the harness straps. This had led to the man's next mistake due to inexperience.

He tried cutting the horse loose from the tangled leather. His son was too small to control the horse, and as the man stumbled in small circles on his crutch, the clumsy handling had frightened the horse even more. The leather harness, slick from the water of the creek, had slipped through the man's hands as the horse took this opportunity to gallop up the bank of the creek and out of sight.

Grady listened, without commenting about a man with a broken leg traveling in this kind of weather, without commenting on all the mistakes the man had made with the horse and the wagon.

"First thing," Grady said, "is we build a fire. There's maybe an hour of daylight left, and I don't aim to get stuck here without one."

Jeremiah cleared his throat cautiously. "Mister O'Neill, what I hoped was you might take my boy home and leave me here. No sense all three of us spending the night in this storm."

"Wouldn't be right," Grady said. "Long's we prepare

right, won't hurt none to wait out this snow. Probably clear up by morning or even sometime in the night."

"Please understand," Jeremiah said, "it ain't me I'm worried for. It's my wife and my other three boys. We went into town yesterday and promised 'em we'd be home by tonight. If we don't show, they'll be scared I'm lost, or something worse."

Lost, Grady wondered. *What kind of man might get lost going home from town?* In his mind, he answered his own question. The same kind of man who'd head out on a day like this, the same kind of man who'd bust an axle, and the same kind of man who'd lose his horse, then wait helplessly on the seat of the wagon.

"Thing is," Jeremiah continued, "I'm afraid my wife might come looking for me. She's strong-minded and would head out with a lantern if she thought it might do some good. I can't see anything but bad happening if she leaves the cabin."

Grady thought it through. Only one horse—his. It could carry a man and a boy, only if Grady removed the mailbags. Even if Grady said he'd stay and guard the wagon and the mailbags, this Sparling fellow wouldn't be able to ride home with his boy, not with that leg busted up like it was.

Jeremiah mistook Grady's silence for reluctance.

"Mister, I can't leave behind my wagon and all the supplies. Cash money's real scarce right now. Anything happens to these supplies, we won't last the winter."

Grady nibbled his lower lip. It was a habit of his when he didn't know what to do.

"Some five miles ahead and directly along the way," Jeremiah told him, "you'll see a rock tower guarded by a tall pine. Turn west, along the trail that follows the creek, and another few miles up is the homestead. With the horse you've got, it would take no time at all to get my oldest boy home and let my family know where I'm at."

Grady kept nibbling his lip. Snow drifted down harder as he thought about the mailbags he needed to take off the horse to make room for the boy.

Chances were he'd lost his job anyway, because a Pony Express man never stopped. This one time, though, might be he could convince folks at Pony Express that he had just cause for stopping. He'd never keep his job, though, if they found out he'd left his mailbags with a stranger.

On the other hand, if he didn't take the boy home, there were the mother and three other boys all alone, worrying about these two. And if the woman did go out into the night . . .

Jeremiah stared anxiously at the Pony Express rider and twisted his hat in his hands. He could see his sweet Grace staring out the window, wondering and waiting. He heard her last words in his mind. He had to find a way to let her know he and the boy were fine.

"We get that fire going," Jeremiah said, doing his best to keep desperation out of his voice, "I'll be fine here waiting. I got blankets and a rifle and food. I don't know what else I can do except throw myself on your mercy."

Grady finally nodded. He decided if the snow let up, someone might track back from the Weyburn ranch and come looking for him. But they had at least twelve or fourteen miles to reach this wagon. So if the snow let up,

Grady would be back well in time to pick up his mailbags before they'd arrive. Chances were, then, no one would ever find out that he'd left them behind.

"Consider it done," Grady said. "I've got to make room for your boy on my horse. That means I need to hide the mailbags in your wagon. What with bank drafts and business letters, I can't tell you how important it is to keep them safe."

What Grady didn't add was that the mailbags were sealed with stamped lead. At least Grady didn't have to worry about the man going through the mail during the night.

"God bless you!" Jeremiah said, then hesitated. "Just in case it takes awhile to ride out the storm, can you deliver some presents? I promised my family something for Christmas, and a man hates breaking promises to his children."

Grady nodded again. Impatiently. The snow was sweeping in harder, and he wanted to be on his way.

The man hobbled around his wagon. He leaned over the side and dug into a box and came back with four small packages, wrapped in plain brown paper, tied with cheap string.

"One for each of my boys," he said. He'd lowered his voice so that Noah couldn't hear.

Grady took them and slipped them inside his coat.

"Thank you kindly," Jeremiah said. "Comes the day I can help you or anyone else, I'll return the favor."

Grady waited. He was expecting Jeremiah to come up with another gift, one for his wife.

Jeremiah half frowned. "Something wrong?"

"I'll be happy to take along the present for your woman," Grady told him.

"We're going through tough times," he said, staring off. "Something little would put a sparkle back in her eyes, but all I could afford was a few trinkets for the boys. I'm hoping she'll understand."

Grady looked off, sorry he'd shamed the man into this admission. He'd gather wood as fast as he could and let the man be.

"Best get the fire going," Grady said, already walking away. "Night like tonight, you're going to need it."

7

Kentucky lay on his belly,
rifle beside him, and watched the wagon activity below
at the creek bed with great interest.

He knew he'd been fortunate that neither the
Pony Express rider nor the man in the floppy hat had
seen him when he first rode up to the edge of the
bank.

Falling snow and fading daylight not only limited the
visibility but covered the sounds of Kentucky's horse.
Kentucky's cause had been further aided because the
Pony Express man had been busy dragging wood toward the wagon, and the man in the floppy hat had
been talking to the boy beside him.

Maybe, Kentucky thought, just maybe their luck had
turned. Them mailbags were sure to have bank drafts

and such, maybe even paper money that folks were sending across the country. Taking them was much easier than robbing a bank.

Even with Reb as terrible sick as he was.

Behind Kentucky were the horses, now tethered well back from the creek bed. Kentucky had tied Reb into the saddle and covered him with a blanket, only because he didn't know what else to do. His brother was barely conscious. Kentucky had himself convinced that all it would take for Reb to get better was the warmth of a fire, some decent food, and a good night's rest.

All three necessities were down below. The fire, it appeared, would be ready in minutes. Supplies were visible in the back of the open wagon. And he and Reb would rest well once Kentucky took the required action to get them the fire and food, for there'd be no one else on this trail tonight, and they'd have at least until morning before they needed to flee. Best of all, if the snow continued, it would hide their tracks.

Yes, sir, Kentucky told himself, their luck was changing. The Pony Express horse stood at the side of the wagon, with the mailbags dangling in sight like ripe apples waiting to be plucked.

First person he'd have to hit, Kentucky decided, was the Pony Express man. Then the man with the busted leg. Kentucky didn't want to have to shoot the boy and wouldn't, not unless the boy went for the gun in the Pony Express man's holster. Although it would have been nice to have Reb at his side, at a distance of less than fifty yards Kentucky probably wouldn't miss.

Kentucky held off on shooting, however, because he saw no sense in hurrying down before all the work was done. One man was fixing a fire and getting wood. The other man was reaching into the supplies for food and blankets. Fact was, Kentucky told himself, he might just wait until they had a meal prepared. The fire would give him enough light to hold a bead on his target.

So Kentucky waited longer, hardly even feeling the cold ground against his belly and legs. Come tomorrow night, he'd be in a hotel, ready to celebrate in a saloon. He'd . . .

Kentucky blinked. It was much darker now, and he

wasn't sure if he saw correctly. The Pony Express man had just unloaded the mailbags off his horse.

Kentucky watched with the concentration of a cougar about to pounce on a deer. He watched the scene unfold, like the best dream he could have hoped for.

The man with the busted-up leg helped the Pony Express man hide the mailbags in the wagon. Then the Pony Express man lifted the boy and put him on the horse's back, directly behind the saddle. The mail agent swung up into the saddle himself, and the boy clutched his arms around the rider. Finally the Pony Express rider and the boy rode off into the snow-filled dusk.

That left a crippled greenhorn guarding the mailbags.

Kentucky grinned.

This was going to be a good Christmas after all.

8

"You know your pa should tell you this," Grace said, her boys gathered around. "He's the one with the stories."

"Tell us evil eye," Seth said.

"Tell us, tell us," Caleb echoed. "Evil eye. Evil eye."

Grace sighed theatrically, and her three boys clapped. They never tired of the story Grace had heard Jeremiah tell the first night they met.

"As you know," Grace said, "your granpa was a doctor in Virginia. So when your pa was your age, Josiah, he sometimes followed his own pa on calls."

"Granny Morris," Seth said. "Granny Morris."

"Yes," Grace said. "Old Granny Morris. Her face was wrinkled so bad a person couldn't ever tell if Granny Morris was grinning or spitting mad. Except most of

SIGMUND BROUWER

the time she was spitting mad. Folks were scared of her. Said she could cast spells. Now one of her neighbors, another old woman by the name of Mrs. Callison, made the mistake of crossing her, so old Granny Morris made a visit to this poor neighbor and gave her the evil eye and said she had cast a spell to grow a frog in her stomach."

Seth giggled. "Frogs grow down by the creek."

"Yes, sir," Grace said, warming up to her story. "Frogs do grow down by the creek. Except Mrs. Callison believed in the spell and in a day or two was certain that she could feel a frog wriggling in her stomach."

"Oooooh," the boys said together, as they always did at this point in the story.

"Now you all know there's no such thing as spells, don't you?"

"Yes, ma'am," all three said.

"All a person needs is faith in the good Lord," Grace said. "Trouble is, sometimes when you believe something, you can make it so. Didn't take but another week and this poor neighbor was lying on her deathbed, convinced that the frog in her stomach was getting bigger and bigger. Your own granpa, he visited every day and couldn't do a thing to help this woman get better. Pills. Potions. Nothing worked."

"Pa knew what to do, didn't he, and he was just a boy," Josiah said. "Pa's a smart man!"

Grace closed her eyes, thinking of her last bitter words to her husband. Jeremiah *was* a smart man. A good schoolteacher. It's just that he wasn't very practical. And this wilderness was no place for a man who couldn't use his hands.

"Yes," Grace said. "Your pa's a smart man. Even though he was just a boy, he knew exactly what to do. When he told your granpa, why that old doctor laughed and laughed. And sure enough, next visit, Doc Sparling gave your pa's idea a try."

Grace continued telling the story, able to picture it in her head from the way Jeremiah always painted stories with words. She recalled his words.

Jeremiah's father, old Doc Sparling, was tall and thin, almost harsh looking, but carried himself gentle and spoke slow, so folks knew he cared. Doc Sparling had first argued with his son that if it worked, the ailing woman might only believe more in the evil eye. Jeremiah argued back, as he always told in his story, that when folks hear how they did it, they'll all know Granny Morris was nothing but an old wind-bag.

Doc had finally agreed, and so it was that both of them pulled up to Mrs. Callison's house.

The bedroom was dark where the old woman lay dying. She'd insisted that the curtains always be drawn, and it had been like that since the day Granny Morris gave her the evil eye and told her a frog was growing in her stomach. On this day, Mrs. Callison was so far gone she could hardly raise her head as Doc Sparling walked up to her bed.

Jeremiah said the old woman's hair was thin and white, and it clung to her head, making her look even thinner than she was. He said she'd happened to catch a fever the day after Granny Morris gave her the evil eye and maybe that's why she started to believe the nonsense about the frog in her stomach.

As Grace continued to retell Jeremiah's story, she could hear the conversation that took place.

"Mrs. Callison," Doc said gravely, with young Jeremiah tagging behind, "it may not be long at all."

She nodded and rested her head back on the pillow.

"But I won't give up," Doc said.

"It ain't no use," Mrs. Callison said. "Not against the evil eye."

"Let's try one last potion," Doc urged. He made a great show of taking an empty glass jar from his medicine bag and setting it on the table beside her bed. "Don't give Granny Morris the pleasure of knowing you went without a fight."

The old woman's face tightened in anger, and she spoke with more firmness. "Doc, give me what you got."

At this point in the retelling, Grace began to giggle. Josiah had guessed correctly in that it might cheer her up.

> *The substance that old Doc Sparling gave next to Mrs. Callison was called ipecac, a vile substance that cleaned a person out. It worked well that afternoon, because, sure enough, Mrs. Callison sent Jeremiah running to get a bedpan because she didn't have the strength to get herself out of bed and to the outhouse.*
>
> *And in the darkness of her room, it was no trouble at all doing the next part, not for Jeremiah, who had been quick enough to catch the frog in the first place. All he'd done at that point was take the frog out of his pocket and give it to Doc as he pulled away the bedpan when Mrs. Callison was finished.*
>
> *"Mrs. Callison!" Doc had shouted with glee. "The operation was a success!"*
>
> *"What?" Mrs. Callison had asked.*
>
> *"Quick, Jeremiah," Doc had said. "Hand me the jar! Before it gets away!"*

Jeremiah had done as requested. In the dimness of the bedroom, Doc had bent over again and made some quick movements hard to distinguish in the dark.

"Just like I figured," Doc had explained as he straightened. He held the jar high where Mrs. Callison could admire it. "We moved that little rascal right out!"

And there it was. A frog in the jar. Just like it had actually left her stomach.

Grace stopped, giggling right along with her boys. How Grace wished Jeremiah were here to finish the story, because his imitation of an old woman was perfect.

Mrs. Callison, as Jeremiah told it, sat up, studied that jar, and watched as the frog bumped into the glass with every hop.

"Doc," Mrs. Callison had said after a few seconds, "now you can see why I was feeling so poorly. A frog that big hopping around inside would kill a mule, let alone an old lady."

As the boys laughed and clapped, Grace carefully looked away toward the window with the burning candle.

She wished so badly that she could hear Jeremiah tell this story again. Didn't matter if he was a romantic fool who could barely hit a nail with a hammer.

She loved him.

9

Even with the snow falling

heavily in the purple light of dusk, Grady had ridden through plenty worse. It was his job, no different than for every other Pony Express man in the country. They weren't to let snow or hail or heat or Indian attacks stop them. It was as simple as that.

The boy, Noah, said nothing for the first half hour as they rode.

The snow began to fall so heavily that the west face of the rock tower was already coated white when they got there. Grady found the dry creek bed easily enough and was grateful for it. The way it was snowing, he needed the dark outline of the rocks to follow.

Because of the terrain and the snow and the boy balanced on the haunches of the horse, he could not ride hard as snow whipped across the horse. Grady's arms and gloves became as white as the ground.

Soon the rocks, too, were covered, and Grady walked the horse even slower.

In silence, the boy clutched Grady's waist.

"You all right?" Grady finally said.

"Yes, sir." That was it from the boy.

As it became darker, Grady found it more difficult to see. He drew back on the reins to stop the horse. Grady swung down.

"Son," he said, "I'm going to have to lead the horse. Slide forward and sit on the saddle. You'll find the horn. Hold on to it tight."

"Yes, sir."

As Grady walked, the leather of his boots became dark with the snow that melted on the warmth of his feet. It didn't take long for his toes to lose this heat and become numb. By Grady's calculations, he still had some several miles to go. At this pace, it would be at least two more hours of walking. As he plodded forward, he thought of Lucy and a warm fire.

Merry Christmas, he told himself. *Thank you, Lord, for a merry, merry Christmas.*

10

Wrapped in a blanket,
Jeremiah sat on a box beside a stack of wood for the
fire. In front of him, flames flickered comfort, and
snow sizzled as it hit the glowing logs.

He stared at a pot of beans and stirred the contents
occasionally by reaching into it with a long stick. But he
wasn't hungry. Not with so many reasons to believe he
didn't belong out here on the Frontier, reasons to
doubt the good Lord's plans for him and his family.

The splint on his right leg was evidence enough. It
had been three weeks earlier that Jeremiah tried work-
ing a horse with a split hoof. Noah had been there to
watch it all. Jeremiah had failed to tie the horse se-
curely. When he touched the horse's hoof with a file,
the horse had bucked hard, slamming Jeremiah into

the post of the pen. Noah had been the one to yank hard on the rope and pull the horse away before it stomped Jeremiah where he lay helpless on the ground. Jeremiah would have been hard-pressed to declare what was worse—the feeling of pain and helplessness on the ground as he waited for one of those thrashing hooves to crush his skull, the fact that he'd been rescued by a son who couldn't look him in the eye anymore, or the sickening sound of his thighbone as it had snapped against the post with the same casual indifference of a wagon axle breaking against stone.

'Course, now the fact was that it had taken another man to rescue him and deliver Noah to Grace and the boys. Jeremiah knew whatever happened was part of God's plan, but he wondered why it had to involve so much pain and humiliation.

He was lost in these thoughts when a man stepped into the light of the fire.

Jeremiah gasped.

The man was huge, with a long coat open to show a revolver holstered on each side of his hips. Long greasy hair hung down from under the sides of the man's hat. The front of the man's long coat was covered with a mixture of mud and snow and some broken, dried grass.

Jeremiah tried to scramble to his feet, but his splinted leg made the efforts futile.

"Evening, pards," the man said. His face was lost in shadow. "Just rest easy. I don't mean no harm. Fact is, I was hoping my brother and I might join you. We've been on the trail some, and this storm has about done us in."

"Yes," Jeremiah said without hesitation. "Definitely yes. No man should have to face this storm. Your brother . . ."

"Back on his horse. Fever's got him bad. If you don't mind, I'll help him set in front of the fire, then unsaddle the horses and join the both of you." This time, the man did not wait for a reply. He disappeared into the wall of snow outside the light of the fire and returned shortly with a smaller man he supported by carrying under the shoulders with one massive arm. In his other arm, the man carried two blankets.

"This here's Reb," the man said. "I'm Kentucky. Pleased to make acquaintance."

"Jeremiah," Jeremiah said. "Jeremiah Sparling."

With a gentleness that Jeremiah found touching from such a fierce-looking man, Kentucky set his brother on the ground.

Kentucky dusted away some snow off the ground near the fire and rolled out a blanket. He lifted his brother and set him on the blanket, then placed the other blanket over top.

Reb's eyes fluttered open briefly, then shut again. The firelight showed beads of sweat across his forehead. His body shook beneath the blanket.

"Looks like the fever's got him real bad," Jeremiah said. "My father was a doctor. I know some about fevers. This man needs something to drink. Water. Tea. Anything that'll replace the sweat he's losing. And we'll need to keep him warm."

Jeremiah struggled to his feet. He shook snow off his blanket and set the blanket on the box.

Jeremiah leaned on his crutch as he spoke to the big man. "I've got some supplies in the wagon. I'll see what I can do. In the meantime, you're welcome to share the beans I've got on the fire."

"Much obliged," Kentucky said. "You're a good man."

"Anybody would do it," Jeremiah said. "Think nothing of it."

"Well, now," Kentucky said, tipping his hat to Jeremiah, "I'll tend to the horses." Again, the big man disappeared quietly into the snow.

As Jeremiah moved to the wagon, he remembered his recent promise to the Pony Express man. *"Comes the day I can help you or anyone else, I'll return the favor."*

Looked like the Lord had granted him the opportunity already. On the eve of Christmas no less.

Jeremiah smiled.

Never let it be said, he thought, that the Lord did not know how to time events properly.

11

Grace was at the stove again,
removing the browned biscuits, when she heard a dog
barking above the wind.

For a heart-stopping moment of hope, she thought
it might be Jeremiah and Noah finally returned. But
she heard no voices to calm the dog or to confirm her
hope.

She glanced across the short distance of the cabin to
where the boys had fallen asleep on their corn-shuck
mattress. None stirred.

Grace gathered her courage and went to the far wall
where a rifle hung, loaded and ready for intruders. She
took it down.

She wondered if she should light a lantern and decided against it. If the intruder had bad intentions—if

indeed there was an intruder—the lantern would only serve to give a target.

Grace hesitated and listened again.

Yes, above the wind, she did hear a noise. Directly outside.

Still no welcome shout from her husband or son.

She grabbed her coat and threw it on. A final glance at her boys. They were asleep.

Grace pushed open the tiny door of the cabin.

Great flakes of snow swirled into the dim light given by the candles. Beyond that, she saw nothing.

But again, a sound reached her.

She was able to identify it.

The snorting of a horse.

She wanted to shout into the wind and snow, but that would wake the boys.

She shut the door behind her, clutching the rifle.

Instantly, her face grew wet from snow that melted on her skin. She blinked against the flakes that collected on her eyelashes.

The snorting of the horse came from behind her.

Cautiously, she began walking farther into the night, away from the safety of the cabin.

As she circled to the side, a dark figure loomed tall in front of her, and she bit back a scream.

12

The fierce wind

down the eastern slopes of the mountains ceased. With the death of the wind, the temperature seemed to be less harsh. While the snow lessened, however, it did not stop completely and drifted down in eerie silence.

Occasionally in the West, as storms die on the night of a full moon, the light of the moon reflects off the snow, so that a white glow fills the night.

This was one of those nights.

The trees were sentinels on each side of the trail that Grady followed, marking his path clearly. He and the boy on the horse appeared like ghostly figures walking on a ghostly night.

"Ever been out on a night like tonight?" Grady asked the boy, not looking back as he spoke.

"No, sir," the boy said.

That was all the boy said. He didn't seem much in-terested in conversation, so Grady didn't push. He was accustomed to long days by himself anyway and didn't need talk to keep him occupied.

Grady lost himself in thought as he led the horse along the trail. It dipped and rose, crossing the creek with regularity.

Grady guessed it was close to seven o'clock. If he reached the cabin by eight o'clock, then turned imme-diately back, he might reach the wagon by ten o'clock. From there, in this light, if Jeremiah was safely settled at the fire and if the wind did not pick up again, he could ride directly to the Weyburn ranch. At most, he might be six hours late.

Forgivable, Grady thought. There had been the odd time or two that Express riders were delayed. Maybe then, Grady decided, he wouldn't lose his job. He could plead that it was Christmas Eve, after all, certainly not a night to abandon a man and a boy in a storm.

Thinking about all of this, Grady's spirits improved.

Inside his coat he had a small bottle of New York perfume wrapped in a silk scarf and ready to give to Lucy Weyburn. Not that he could buy her heart, but he had taken the effort to find out what perfume she liked and had ordered it in the fall.

Grady pictured her wide, warm smile as she opened the gift. He imagined her throwing her arms around him as she hugged him in delight.

Maybe, Grady thought, this Christmas would be fine after all.

Less than a minute of assuring himself of this, Grady led the horse yet again across the creek.

Because it was night, and because so much snow had fallen, and because the snow still filled the air, he could not see that downstream a beaver dam had pooled the water here. Furthermore, the snow had covered the thin layer of ice on top of this pool.

Grady stepped forward to cross the creek and fell through the ice.

13

"Need some help?"

Kentucky hollered from where he was squatted in front of the fire warming his hands.

"No, sir," Jeremiah said. "This snow's making it difficult for me to see what I'm doing."

Jeremiah stood awkwardly at the side of the wagon. He'd glanced at the horses belonging to the men and now made sure to continue loudly enough for Kentucky to hear him. "Why don't you go ahead and get a start on those beans. There's plenty more and I'm digging for them right now, along with another pot and some tea for your brother."

Kentucky didn't waste any time getting started on the beans. He hadn't eaten in a day and a half, and that had been the last of their buffalo jerky. He hadn't eaten anything warm in near a week, not since they'd been on the run with the army horses.

"Hey, brother, save some for me." This came from Reb, who had revived in the heat of the fire. "Those beans smell good."

Jeremiah made plenty of noise as he dug through his supplies. He wished his rifle were down among the contents of the wagon instead of up on the buckboard, where both of these men would notice if he limped over to get it. Maybe Jeremiah was imagining things— it was a habit of his—but these two strangers rode horses with army brands, and they sure didn't look military. Plus, there was the fact that the front of the man's coat had been so dirty, like he'd been lying on his belly. Watching Jeremiah from up top the bank? Jeremiah wasn't about to accuse them of anything, but he wished he weren't crippled and that he carried a pistol. Especially with the promise he'd made to the Pony Express rider about guarding those mailbags.

Jeremiah took so long bent over and moving supplies around in the wagon that the big man shouted again.

"Hey, pards! Need help?"

"Just done now," Jeremiah said. And he was.

Jeremiah finally retrieved a pot and scooped snow into it before hobbling back over to the fire.

"This ought to get your blood going again," Jeremiah said to Reb. "I'll brew some tea and add plenty of sugar."

"Thanks," Reb croaked. "You're a good man."

Kentucky frowned. He didn't want Reb to get feeling too grateful. There was a job to be done tonight.

*   ❄   *

In that same second, out there alone in the dark away from the cabin farther than she'd intended to venture, Grace recognized the figure as a horse. Without a saddle.

She ran back to the cabin and found her lantern, then returned to where the horse waited patiently for some hay.

When she held the light up to the animal, it confirmed her worst fears. It was their horse. No Jeremiah. No Noah.

She shouted into the drifting snow, knowing while she shouted that it was futile.

Their horse had once been harnessed to the wagon. Now it was not. Somewhere, out there in the storm, Jeremiah and Noah were alone.

Her poor foolish and romantic husband. This was what his dream of the West had come to. She dared not wonder if they were alive or dead.

14

"Ma?"

Caleb had woken as Grace came back in the cabin. He was on his elbows, blinking away his grogginess.

"Hush, now," she said softly, moving to the bed. "You just sleep."

She leaned over and kissed his forehead. The other two had not stirred. She loved watching the innocence of her boys' faces as they slept.

"When's Pa and Noah coming home?"

"Hush, now," she repeated just as softly. "Sleep and dream some sweet dreams for your ma."

Grace kissed his forehead again and gently pressed him back on the bed between his brothers. She pulled up the disturbed blanket and covered the three of them again.

She watched as she waited for Caleb's breathing to become long and regular.

Her heart ached as she gazed at her three boys.

If they were still in Chicago, they'd be able to go to school. She wouldn't have to worry about bears and cougars. Jeremiah would have his job as a teacher, and there wouldn't be evenings when the pots were scraped clean of food and the boys still asking for more. She'd have dresses and fine gloves and some nice hats. There'd be church services and friends to chat with, and there would be no spiders crawling in her bedsheets and no smoke to burn her eyes when it filled the cabin and . . .

And if only God hadn't done this to her.

In that moment, Grace realized how angry her thoughts had become.

She took a deep breath and admonished herself. A good wife and a good Christian did not get angry at God.

With a heavy sigh, Grace moved away from the bed and walked to the window. She couldn't see anything but snow, of course, but she did not know where else to look.

Should she go into the night and look for them? Maybe they were just a mile down the trail. Maybe just two. What if all they needed was the light of the lantern to get them home? What if they froze to death out there, and she discovered they had made it almost as far as the doorstep to the cabin? She'd never forgive herself.

No, she told herself firmly. She'd have just as much a chance of getting lost herself as finding them. She could just as easily freeze to death herself. It wasn't her own life she cared about nearly as much as her boys.

Terrible as it might be to lose her husband and oldest son, how much more terrible would it be if she died too, leaving the three young boys with no family?

A more horrible thought hit her. What if she got lost and froze to death and the three boys here died because no one came looking for them? That thought drove away any other notions about going into the storm to look for Jeremiah and Noah.

She sat down and buried her head in her hands. She felt her body shake. For so long she had tried to be so strong. Now the weight of all her fears fell on her hard, as if the burden she'd been carrying for so long had suddenly become unbearable with these new fears.

Oh, God, she thought. *Oh, God.* Like a little girl again, she wept. In her brokenness, she found herself praying again, praying with her heart, not just her words.

Lord, Grace prayed, *please be with them. Please give me the strength to be a good mother and a better wife.*

She opened her eyes and saw the Christmas tree.

She closed her eyes again.

Lord, she prayed, *thank you for sending your Son into this world. Thank you for the hope that I have in life and death because of it.*

Hardly knowing she had begun, Grace began to sing softly.

"Silent night, holy night . . ."

15

As Grady plunged

down into the shock of icy water, he clutched on to the reins of his horse. A yell of surprise left his throat.

The horse smelled the water and the danger it represented. Grady's scream of fear galvanized it to scramble backward. Grady kept firm hold of the reins and let the horse pull him out of the water, marshaling himself to push free from the greasy mud and sediment of the creek bottom.

Just like that, it was over. In less than several heartbeats, he'd broken through ice, half submerged, and then struggled out again.

The horse reared in continued panic, throwing Noah off the saddle.

"Roll!" Grady shouted at the boy. "Away from its feet!"

The boy did as commanded.

The boy's movement, however, caused the horse to rear higher and snort in terror.

Grady did not panic himself. He wrapped the rein harder around his fist and dodged the front feet of the horse as it came down again and again.

If the horse went, so did Grady's life and perhaps the boy's. For a lost horse meant that Grady would not be able to get at a pouch on his saddle. And this pouch held the most important thing in Grady's life at this moment.

Matches.

Grady yanked the reins hard, bringing the horse's head down. He threw the glove off his free hand and jammed his thumb and forefinger into the horse's nostrils. He squeezed hard and twisted the tender part of the horse's nose. It was an old trick that Grady had learned while breaking horses; the intense pain of it could bring a horse down to its knees.

Grady kept the horse still this way until it no longer struggled.

Grady released the grip and kept the horse's head low with the reins. He soothed it by rubbing its neck.

"You all right, boy?" he asked, not looking over his shoulder to see where Noah had gone.

"Yes, sir," Noah said. The boy stood close behind him. "I didn't land hard at all."

"Glad to hear it," Grady said.

That, at least, was one problem he did not need to address.

Grady kept stroking the horse's neck. When he was finally certain the horse had been calmed, he led it to a tree.

Already Grady was shivering badly. His entire lower body was soaking wet. He'd heard of men dying from loss of heat like this. He needed to get another fire going—and quickly.

The boy had followed him.

"Noah," Grady said. "What I need you to do is break small dried branch tips off these nearby pine trees. Get me as many pieces as you can, as quickly as you can."

Without a word, the boy darted into the trees.

Grady tethered the horse to the tree, struggling against cold that seemed to reach the core of his body.

He moved to the saddle. His hands shook as he fumbled with the straps of his pouch. It held several candles, jerked beef, and a tin tube with a screw cap to keep matches from water.

Well away from the horse, Grady found a flat spot and kicked it free of snow.

Already the boy had returned with the twigs.

"Good," Grady said. "Now get bigger branches."

Again, the boy disappeared without saying anything.

Grady formed the twigs into a small pyramid; then he, too, went in search of branches. He arrived with an armful at the same time as the boy.

Grady's teeth chattered as he knelt beside the twigs. Around this small pyramid he built a larger pyramid of branches and then a larger one on top of that.

He tried to strike a match but couldn't.

"Let me," Noah said.

Grady simply nodded.

The boy knelt beside him, lit the match and then the

candle from the match. He held the candle to the pine twigs in the center of the stacked branches. They snapped into flame. The smaller branches caught quickly, and then the larger branches above those.

"Thanks," Grady said, but he was speaking to no one. The boy had already gone away in search of more wood.

The snow continued to fall.

16

"If you don't mind
passing time during a long cold night," Jeremiah said, "I
can tell you about the laziest cowboy to ride the range.
Works for the Bar X Bar, an outfit next valley over."

"I'd like that," Reb said. "Might take my mind off
what ails me so bad."

Kentucky merely grunted. His belly was full, and he
already had it in his mind that he wanted to kill this
greenhorn and get moving with the mailbags. The wind
had stopped and if the snow stopped next, it'd be too
easy to track them.

Jeremiah poured another coffee and handed it to
Kentucky.

All right then, Kentucky told himself, it wouldn't
hurt to sit a little longer where it was warm.

"Go on," Kentucky said. "Tell us about this here lazy cowboy."

"I worked the roundup with the Bar X Bar last fall," Jeremiah said. "This cowboy by the name of Big Jim had a troublesome habit of napping in the shade of the chuck wagon while the rest of us did the work."

Under his blanket, Reb propped himself up on one elbow. He coughed a few times, and his eyes were shiny in the firelight. He shivered some but gave Jeremiah his full attention.

"It was a hot day," Jeremiah continued, "and Big Jim had made the mistake of removing his boots and socks and rolling up his pants to cool his feet. So the cook sent some of the boys looking for a tarantula. I asked him why, and he told me to wait and watch. Said he was mixing some medicine."

"They was gonna put the tarantula in his britches?" Reb asked. He laughed and coughed some more. "That'd be something all right. But wouldn't Big Jim wake whilst they was fooling with him?"

Jeremiah smiled at the childlike interest of the man

under the blanket. "No spider in his britches." He shook his head for emphasis, and snow fell from the brim of his hat. "Fact is, they let Big Jim sleep sound until the boys got back to camp with a big tarantula. They killed it and laid it down close to Big Jim's foot."

"That wouldn't do no good," Reb said. "How's that—"

"Shut your yap," Kentucky said, interested in spite of himself. "Let the man talk."

"What they did next," Jeremiah said, "was they got a pin and fastened it to the end of a stick and gave Big Jim a couple of jabs in the calf of his leg. Which brought Big Jim up in a hurry, just in time for him to see the tarantula before one of the boys stepped on it and mashed it good, and sure enough, Big Jim believed he'd been bit."

"Say it ain't so," Reb said, grinning wide.

"Sure as we're sitting here right now. Well, Big Jim went hollering to the cook, who informed Big Jim it was a bad case, as more than one man's died to the tarantula."

Jeremiah smiled again. "Wish you could have seen it. All of us gathered round and shaking our heads and telling Big Jim it was good to know him and did he have any last words. And Big Jim just about in tears, waiting for the poison to swell him up like we promised."

"Did he die?" Reb asked.

"He didn't get bit," Kentucky snapped. "If you listened, you'd a heard the man say they jabbed him with a pin and played like the tarantula bit him."

"Yup," Reb said. "I knew that."

Jeremiah continued. "Big Jim begged and begged for someone to help save him. Cook said he knew some Indian potions, if Big Jim wanted to give that a try. Big Jim about fell to his knees in gratitude. So the cook gave him a pint of bear's oil, then a package of soda, a half tea-cup of vinegar, and a quart of water in which he'd been soaking a ten-cent cut of tobacco. Big Jim ate and drank it all as fast as you and me might eat a good piece of steak after four days with no grub. Wasn't much of a surprise that he got as sick as a man could be."

Reb's grin split his face. "That's something all right."

"Don't end there," Jeremiah said. "Big Jim complained to the cook, who asked him to imagine how much worse it'd be without those Injun cures and told Big Jim he owed the cook and the boys a two-gallon jug of whiskey for saving his life. Wasn't till after all the boys drank all the whiskey that they let Big Jim in on the joke. And you can bet your last dollar Big Jim never slept under no wagon again."

Even Kentucky couldn't help smiling.

Sort of sad, Kentucky thought, that he'd have to plug the man before the snow stopped falling.

17

Grace's singing woke Josiah.

He crawled out from under the blanket and stood beside her. He took her hand and held it as he sang with her.

In her vulnerability, this small act of love nearly brought Grace to tears again, but she didn't want to upset Josiah, so she poured her emotion into the Christmas carol.

Josiah kept on, his sweet little voice breaking on the higher notes.

Within minutes, Caleb and Seth had left the blanket.

In the heat of the cabin, all four of them stood near the window, singing to the candlelight that reflected off the glass. Outside the snow fell, but inside they were cozy.

When they finished, Grace felt a peace that surprised her. *God is good,* she realized. *He gives us his love reflected through the love they shared this night.*

Tomorrow would bring what it might. She prayed that Jeremiah and Noah would be returned to her for Christmas, but in this moment, she felt secure in God's love.

Caleb tugged on her hand, taking her out of her thoughts. "'Nuther song?" he asked.

Grace hugged him. "No," she said. "Presents."

"Presents! Presents!"

Grace left them at the window and came back with the hard-rock candy that she had wrapped in plain brown paper.

The boys tore the paper apart and whooped with joy. "Hard-rock candy!"

Grace didn't know what she'd have to give them tomorrow, but their glee made her early gifts worthwhile.

When they gathered around her again, Caleb asked once more. "Songs?"

Grace shook her head and smiled.

"Let me tell you about baby Jesus. . . ."

18

"What was it that you done to the horse?"
Noah asked. He had just returned with more wood for
the fire. These were about the first words he'd spoken
to Grady, aside from "yes, sir" and "no, sir."

"The horse?" Grady said, surprised that the boy had
broken a long silence. "Tethered him to the tree."

"I mean when it was bucking," Noah said, setting the
wood down and feeding a few pieces to the fire. "You
done something to him."

Snow still fell. A half hour had passed. The fire
burned briskly. Grady stood barefoot on a blanket he
had unrolled in front of the fire. His socks and boots
were off, so close to the heat of the fire that steam rose
from the cotton and leather.

In his coat and long underwear, Grady held his pants

in front of him on the end of a short, stout branch. He'd been turning it back and forth in the heat of the fire. In another half hour or so, he figured, the pants would be dry enough he could continue without worrying about freezing to death.

Grady lifted his eyes from the fire and turned his gaze to the boy.

Noah had a serious, quizzical look on his face.

"Pinch your nose as hard as you can," Grady said. "Then twist. See if it hurts."

The boy tried it and quit immediately.

Grady had hoped for a smile but did not get it.

"Hurts, huh?" Grady said. "When you do it to a horse, it's even worse. How much do you weigh?"

"Sixty pounds," the boy answered calmly, not rattled by the change of subject.

"And a horse might weigh eight hundred. Even so, small as you are compared to a horse, you could control it completely by jamming a thumb in one nostril, a finger in the other, and twisting. When you do that, it won't even prance."

"Thank you," Noah said. "I'll remember that."

"And if you're riding a horse and it's taken off in a gallop and you lose your reins, there's another trick."

The boy waited in serious silence.

"What you do," Grady said, "is lean forward, wrap your arms around its neck, and bite through one of its ears and hold tight until it stops."

"You funnin' me?"

"Not at all. It might save your life someday. You never want to be on a runaway horse. It steps in a hole and throws you, you might snap your neck like kindling."

"Thank you," Noah said. "I'll remember that."

Grady studied the boy.

Noah had taken off his hat in front of the fire. His hair was cut short and ragged, making his face look round.

"How old are you?" Grady asked.

"Eleven."

"Why is it that you are so determined to learn all this and remember it?"

For a moment, Noah didn't answer.

Then, when he spoke, he stared at his feet. "My pa,

he needs help, I figure. Seems like other men around here don't hurt themselves or get lost or build things that fall over the next day. They don't drive a wagon in a creek and break the axle and wait for someone to come by. My pa . . ."

Grady sensed this was difficult for the boy to say. So Grady didn't interrupt; he just waited.

"Ma called my pa a fool. She said he brung us out here to get us all killed. Said he should have stayed in Chicago and kept his job in a schoolhouse instead of spending all we had to follow a crazy dream of his."

Noah finally looked up at Grady. "So I figure I better learn what I can. It was me that chopped and stacked all our firewood for the winter. Pa, he'd be off by himself, sitting in the sun with a drawing pad and a quill and ink, and I'd make sure the work got done."

Noah looked back down again at his feet.

Grady understood. The boy was ashamed of his own father.

19

Kentucky stood away from the fire.

It was time to get his rifle from the horse.

"If you don't mind," Jeremiah said, wrapped in his blanket, staring at the flames, "I'd like to tell you another story. The best story a man could hear."

Reb nodded from the other side of the fire. He was sitting up now, caped by his blanket, snow on his shoulders and hat.

Kentucky shook his head. "Never was much for stories," he said.

"I'd like to hear it," Reb said. "Set a spell. We ain't got anywhere to go."

Kentucky sat again. He wanted to shake his brother. Of course they had somewhere to go. Reb didn't know it, but there were those mailbags waiting for them in the wagon. All they needed to do was make sure they didn't leave a witness behind. And the sooner the better. Who knew when that Pony Express rider might return and complicate this?

"You boys might appreciate this," Jeremiah said, "for it looks like you've spent your share of time on the trail. Anyway, there was this man and woman lived in a land a long time ago and far away. Her belly was big, and she was real close to having her baby, and there they were, with no place to rest. It was a cold night, maybe not snowing like now, but a cold night and nobody would help them out. So they stopped for the night in a stable. And right there, she had her baby. Now this baby was born to save the world."

"I heard this before," Kentucky growled. "Let me tell you, I don't see that the world needs saving."

"Hush," Reb said. "I want to hear him out. This man knows how to tell a story."

Jeremiah turned his face to Kentucky. "I'll agree it might seem like the world doesn't need saving, but did you ever get shivers when you heard a coyote howl at night? You ever felt that same kind of sadness looking up at the sky filled with stars? You ever been homesick, not knowing where it was you wanted to be?"

Reb shivered and huddled beneath his blanket. "I been lonely lots."

"What it is," Jeremiah said, "is that God's put a place in your soul that will always feel empty until you let him fill it."

"This ain't a place for a sermon," Kentucky grunted.

"No sermon," Jeremiah said. "But a man should spend time thinking why he's been put on this earth. Reb, you're tired and sick, and that's a terrible place to be. Ever want some place you can just sit and rest and not worry and just be filled with peace that lets you know you're where you should be in this world?"

"Plenty," Reb said. Beneath his beard, he was just a boy, and at this moment he was so weak that he allowed himself to feel his loneliness. "Last time I had that kind of peace, it was when my ma would hold me tight when I was a little boy. Seems since then that . . ."

"Reb . . . ," Kentucky warned, "she died a long time ago. We don't talk about her to strangers."

Reb shut his mouth. Kentucky stared at the fire. Jeremiah let the silence hang for a few minutes.

"I'm truly sorry about your ma," Jeremiah began again. "Hurts bad, losing someone you love. And to me, that's why the world needs saving. This baby that was born, he was meant to take away all that hurt and fill it with love straight from God, and not only that, make sure you could get to heaven and see your ma again. Fact is, that's why the angels showed up that night and started singing to shepherds in the nearby fields."

"Angel music," Reb said, his voice soft. "Can't imagine anything purtier."

"It would have been some night," Jeremiah agreed. "All because of God's gift to you and me, this baby Jesus . . ."

And so Jeremiah continued.

20

"This baby Jesus,"

Grace said to her three boys, "he lay there in the manger so sweet. Then arrived these wise men, who had followed a star rising in the East, because the star told all the world about this wonderful event."

Her boys listened, enthralled. She sat with them on their corn-shuck mattress. She was still filled with the peace that had entered the small cabin as they had sung their carols.

"The wise men were accustomed to advising kings and other great rulers," she said. "They knew this baby would be the greatest ruler of all. And they were right."

Her boys pressed up against her, and again she uttered a silent prayer of thanks to God for allowing her these precious gifts of life and love.

"Oh, he wasn't the kind of king who sat on a throne and ordered people here and there," Grace said softly. She found herself telling the boys the Christmas story the way Jeremiah always told it. "When Jesus grew up, he didn't care much about money. He traveled through that same land, showing people how much he loved them. He healed them when they were sick and he fed them when they were hungry and he told them again and again how much God loved all of them."

Grace smiled at her boys. "And Jesus tells us how much God loves us too. Because God has a home for all of us. He's waiting for you and me, and all we have to do is listen to Jesus and pray to God. That's the best Christmas present ever."

"Better than hard-rock candy?" Seth asked.

"Much better," Grace said. She smiled at each of her boys in turn. "If someone asked me if I wanted hard-rock candy or the three of you to love, I'd tell them that love is much, much better than hard-rock candy or money or a big house. Wouldn't you agree?"

As an answer they each hugged her.

Looking over their heads, Grace saw the candle at the window again.

She didn't let go of her boys until she had managed to blink away her fresh tears.

21

Draped with fresh snow,
branches of the trees along the wagon trail were
sculpted angels, watching in silence as Grady and the
boy rode the final mile toward the cabin.

The snow had finally stopped falling. The full moon
shone now that the clouds had cleared, reflecting off
the whiteness of the landscape. Night was almost
brighter than the gray of the afternoon earlier. Grady
easily saw ahead, and he knew his return journey to the
wagon and then to the ranch would not be difficult.

He felt no peace about it, however. The quietness of
the boy behind him was like a burden. It didn't take
much effort for Grady to imagine how it would be for
any boy to feel shame about his father. He felt bad for
the boy.

On the surface, it seemed the boy had good reason. On first arriving at the wagon, Grady, too, had been quick in his mind to accuse the settler of incompetence.

Then one single thought about Jeremiah popped into Grady's mind. The man, at least, has plenty of courage to be out here without knowing where life might take him.

Grady chewed on that thought for some ten minutes before he was ready to speak. He knew he had to say it right. Every boy deserved to be able to respect his father, and it seemed like Grady was at the right place and right time to be able to help.

"I remember the first time I rode a horse," Grady began, speaking into the quiet of the night. "My daddy didn't think I was old enough, so I snuck into the barn and saddled it myself. I jumped on that horse and rode proud. Until just down the road me and that saddle slid right off the horse. Turned out I hadn't buckled the saddle right."

No response from Noah.

"'Course," Grady said, "it *was* my first time. Should I be blamed for not getting it right?"

"No, sir." The boy spoke so quietly, Grady barely heard him. "A person has to learn."

"Exactly," Grady said. "You can bet I never made that mistake again. Because I did just that. I learned. Shoot, unless there was someone right there to show him, every man in this Territory has learned what he learned the hard way. Including me."

"Yes, sir."

Grady let the horse walk farther. Each breath of the horse rose as white vapor in the still night air.

"There's a girl waiting for me tonight at a ranch," Grady said. "She's been stuck on me a long time. I believe she's hoping I might someday ask her to marry me."

This time, when Grady paused, Noah did not reply.

Of course, Grady realized, the poor boy might be perplexed as to why Grady was telling him this.

"Thing is," Grady continued, "I'm afraid. I can rope a steer, break a horse, build a fence, shoot as good as the next man, and I'm afraid to go somewhere in my life that's new to me. I've been a lone man for quite some time, and I'm accustomed to it. Changing to a married man, that's quite a jump, and I'm not sure I can make it."

Grady was glad he could not see the face of the boy behind him. This way, it was like Grady was just thinking out loud, finally admitting to himself something he'd tried to keep hidden from his heart.

"Over the last few years," he confessed, "I've taken just about any job that would give me an excuse not to settle down. Including this one for the Pony Express. In so doing, I've treated that woman poorly. I stay just close enough she can't say good-bye, and just far enough I can't say 'I do.' It's been right handy, having a sweetheart without having the responsibility."

Grady whistled. "And having children? That's enough to make me faint with fear. What if she died giving birth? What if one of my children took sick and died? What if I died and left them alone with no one to support them? There's so many things that could go wrong, it's just plain and simple much easier not to try. A man could grow old and never take a chance like that and live just fine. I know plenty who've done it that way."

Wood smoke reached Grady's nostrils. They were close to the cabin.

He stopped the horse and stepped down. He wanted to look the boy in the face for what he had to say next. "Noah, you probably don't know where I'm going with this, so I'll spell it out."

Noah looked down at him gravely.

"Don't hold it against your pa that he's not a man of the territories yet. Most of us out here have spent years learning what we need to know. Give your pa time; he'll do just fine. Remember, if you haven't done it before, there's no shame in making mistakes."

Grady made sure he gazed square into Noah's eyes. "Your pa, he's a brave man. Not many would leave behind something they're good at to try their hand at something unfamiliar. It's a lesson I'm going to learn from him. Tomorrow I'm going to propose to Lucy and take a chance on family and following dreams, just like your pa has done. I only hope I'm half the man your pa is."

Grady let that hang there in the silence, keeping Noah's gaze.

Finally, the boy nodded.

Then smiled.

22

"Near the end,"

Jeremiah said, "there was the three of them, each hanging on a cross. Soldiers had nailed them hand and foot."

Although he hadn't meant to go on so long, from the beginning of the gospel story, he'd told it through almost to the end. About the lepers and the fathers who begged him to heal their children and the blind man and the pigs that jumped off the cliff. It seemed to Jeremiah that Reb had an innocent desperate hunger for the stories, so it was just natural to keep going, even with Kentucky shifting impatiently at the side of the fire, occasionally getting up to wander to the horses then wandering back again to the fire.

"Nailed to the cross?" Reb said. "Ain't right. Sure

them two, they was robbers; they deserved it. But him, he never did nothing but try to help people. And didn't say a word to defend himself."

Jeremiah stirred the fire with a stick. Embers flew into the air.

"That's why Christmas is so special, Reb," Jeremiah said. "If that baby hadn't been born, he would never have gotten to that cross."

"Just to die?"

"To die for me," Jeremiah said quietly. "And for you. Right where you're lying, that man died for you to fill that emptiness you have. Because he loved you like a father loves his son. Believe that Jesus was sent from God and believe in his message and ask him to take you home to him, and you'll have peace, no matter what happens in your life, good times and bad."

"I ain't good enough to have someone die for me," Reb said. He shivered. "Trust me on that."

"Let me tell you the end of it," Jeremiah said. "Then you decide. See, people were yelling at Jesus on the cross, and one of those robbers said just what you did.

That it wasn't right. And Jesus looked at him with all that love and told him that very day he would be in heaven with Jesus. No matter what a person's done wrong, God loves him, and all it takes is to ask forgiveness."

Reb hugged himself beneath his blanket, staring thoughtfully at the fire. "And the other fellow on the cross. The other thief?"

"Didn't feel bad at all," Jeremiah said. "Not for Jesus. Not for himself. He died with a hardened heart."

Reb closed his eyes. They stayed closed so long that Jeremiah wondered if Reb's fever had taken him again.

Kentucky rose from the fire yet one more time and walked toward their horses. The snow was so soft his steps made no noise.

Eyes still closed, Reb spoke as if he were speaking to himself. "I'm so tired. So very tired." He opened them again. "Sure wish I could have been there," he said, "hearing all that angel music."

Reb's voice got quieter and weaker as the fever began to take him away again. "Knowing all this about what that baby done and become when he growed into a man, I'd have been right up front, singing with the best of them."

23

When Jeremiah had busted his leg and Grace had been nursing him through the first few nights, he'd turned to her and said, just once in those sleepless nights, that if he ever died, he hoped she might look through his drawing pads, which he kept hidden under the mattress, and send his stories to someone who might put them in a book.

Grace hadn't given that request much thought at the time. She doubted he was going to die. She had the four boys and a household to run. She'd been busy nursemaiding Jeremiah. There had been no opportunities to sit and wonder about what he'd kept secret and why.

Now, with the fire burning, the candle in the window almost a stub, and the boys back asleep, his request came to her mind. Send his stories to someone who might put them in a book.

Grace climbed the loft to their bed. The loft was just a platform in the rafters, and there was little room to stand, but she was always grateful for the relative privacy this gave them.

Under the mattress she found his drawing pad.

The light up in the loft was too dim for her to see what he had written. She took it down near a lantern and lifted the cover of the drawing pad.

The yellow light showed a delightful sketch of an old woman's face, her cheeks like prunes, her hair wild like a nest of snakes. Underneath in bold lettering was a single phrase: *Evil Eye.*

So this was his secret dream. Taking stories and putting them on paper.

Thinking that Jeremiah might already be dead, Grace put a hand to her mouth and bit her knuckle. Her poor, sweet husband, spending time on this, too afraid to let her know.

Grace flipped to the next page. As a schoolteacher,

Jeremiah had always been a stickler for good handwriting, and she was able to clearly read each word.

> *"Suzy!" I hissed that hot summer afternoon in our small Virginia town. "You git yourself out from behind that pickle barrel!"*
>
> *"C'ain't," she hissed back. "She's here! I don't want the evil eye."*
>
> *"How many times do I have to tell you—" I cut myself short and grinned weakly at Granny Morris as she leaned on her cane and wobbled her way toward me down the store aisle. "Fine day, ma'am."*
>
> *Granny Morris glared at me. At least I think it was a glare. Hardly any light made it here in back of Guthrie's General Store. And with enough light, her old face was wrinkled so bad a person couldn't ever tell if Granny Morris was grinning or spitting mad.*
>
> *"Josh Callison," she said, "you get that egg-sucking grin off your face. I despise you as much as the rest of your kin."*

Grace giggled. She could hear Jeremiah telling it this way. What a delight, seeing it in words on paper. She resumed reading and began to get lost in the story.

> Granny Morris turned her head and spit a blob of tobacco juice onto the rough wood floor. "Fact is, boy, I might decide to cast a spell on you too."
>
> Suzy whimpered from her hiding position behind the pickle barrel.
>
> "You don't scare me none." She did, but I had to say it loud for Suzy to hear. Suzy was eight and needed a man of twelve like me to look after her. "I don't believe in your evil eye."
>
> Granny Morris cackled. "That so, boy? Then you tell me why your gram's lying on her deathbed. It learned her good, didn't it, for spreading word that I were an old witch."
>
> I had nothing to reply to that. Gram was only a couple of days away from dying. She said it, and so did Doc Martin. And too many folks agreed it was Granny Morris and her evil eye that caused it.

"Cat got your tongue, boy?" Granny Morris cack-
led louder at my nervous silence. "I might go home
right now and cast a spell to grow a frog in your stomach too!"

That was too much for Suzy. With a shriek . . .

Barking of the dog interrupted Grace's reading.

Her heart leapt with sudden joy.

Only to turn to pain when she opened the door to see
a stranger.

24

Grady stood in the doorway.

A pretty woman with a tired face and worried smile watched him from inside. Behind her, he saw the heads of three boys. She shooed them, and they returned to peek around her. Grady guessed the oldest to be eight years old.

"Hello," the woman said. Her eyes moved up and down as she looked at the snow that covered his hat and coat. She stepped back from the doorway. "Come in. You must be freezing. We've got some soup and you're welcome to it."

"Thank you kindly, but no," he said. "My name's Grady, and I ride for the Pony Express. Your husband—"

She brought her hands to her face. "He's not hurt!

We've been waiting on him, singing Christmas carols to pass time and—"

"He's fine, ma'am. And your oldest boy came with me."

"But Noah . . ."

"Tending to your horse. He saw that it was here and wanted to make sure it was fed."

The woman smiled. "Just like Noah. Always taking care of things."

Grady explained the rest of it, telling Grace about the accident and that Jeremiah was safe at the wagon.

"That sets me at ease," she said. Still, her face looked tired and sad.

Grady took off a snowy glove and pulled a brown package from inside his jacket.

"He asked me to deliver this in case he didn't make it here by tomorrow," Grady said. She smiled as if he had handed her a bar of gold.

"Merry Christmas," Grady said, giving her the other three packages. "He had all of these for the boys."

"Merry Christmas," she said back to Grady. Her eyes kept going to his coat. But Grady didn't have anything for her.

"Well," Grady said, "I've got to be moving on. Can't let the storm get the best of me."

25

Jeremiah sat at the fire.

Snow had begun to fall again.

Reb was in a fitful tossing sleep under the blanket on the other side of the fire.

And when Kentucky walked back to the fire from the horses for the final time, he had the mailbags thrown over his left shoulder and his Winchester in his right hand.

"Sorry, pards," he said to Jeremiah. Kentucky flipped the Winchester so that, waist high, it pointed directly at Jeremiah's chest as he sat in front of the fire. "Couldn't help but see these saddlebags right on top of your supplies. What they've got inside, I need bad. So I'll be moving on."

"But—"

"I'm going to have to shoot you so I can load my brother on his horse and not worry about you making a play to stop me. Can't leave no witnesses behind, neither. Maybe I'd have done you a bigger favor shooting you from behind so you couldn't see it coming, but after hearing your sermon tonight, I thought you might want a chance to say your final prayers before you meet your maker."

Jeremiah sat motionless. He did not beg, merely stared into the rifle barrel.

"Hurry up now," Kentucky said. "Say them prayers."

Jeremiah closed his eyes. "Lord, thank you for sending Jesus so that I may now go to the home you have prepared for me. Please give comfort to Grace and the boys. And, Lord, please be with this man's soul. He needs you. In the name of Jesus I pray. Amen."

Kentucky spit in anger. "You had no call to throw in that part about me."

Jeremiah calmly gazed at the big man.

A sharp metallic click broke the short silence between Jeremiah's prayer and the roar of the Winchester that was to come.

"Shoot him," Reb croaked from behind them, "and I'll have to shoot you, Kentucky. And don't turn neither, or I'll plug you before you get halfway round to facing me."

Jeremiah's eyes shifted to Reb from the big man frozen in surprise above him.

Reb had thrown aside his top blanket. As best he could, he held a wavering revolver with both hands and pointed at Kentucky's back.

"You can't shoot me," Kentucky said. "I'm your brother."

"You ain't gonna kill this man. Drop the rifle."

"All right then," Kentucky said. He let the rifle fall, then slowly turned to face his brother. "Now that you're feeling this spry, let's ride. I've got the mailbags and all the Pony Express mail."

"No," Reb said. "Drop the mailbags too. I'm through with this life."

"I ain't," Kentucky said after several moments. "Fair

enough. I didn't shoot this man. But I'm leaving with these mailbags, and the only way you're gonna stop me is by shooting me."

Kentucky stepped out of the firelight toward his horse. Two more steps into the darkness, he turned around again.

"Brother," Kentucky said, "come with me. I'm the only family you got. And finally, we got some money."

"If you're gonna go," Reb said, his voice shaky, using all his strength to hold the pistol, "git."

When Kentucky was well gone, Reb collapsed again into his fever.

26

The boys were listening

on their bed as Noah recounted all his exciting events.

Grace smiled and let them be. She lit a new candle and placed it in the window.

She sat near the stove with Jeremiah's drawing pad on her lap. She did not continue to read, however, but sat and stared at the candle and thought.

She admonished herself first for her initial disappointment over the Christmas gifts. She should have been proud of Jeremiah for thinking of the boys.

Her Christmas gift was the fact that the stone shell around her heart had cracked and broken and fallen away. It was that Jeremiah was alive and well. God had given her the chance to tell Jeremiah again how much she loved him. God had given her the chance to make up for the mean words she'd spoken before Jeremiah left for town.

As she stared at the drawing pad in her lap, she realized that this evening had given her another gift. New respect for her husband.

She remembered what she had said to her boys earlier in the evening while telling them the story about Old Granny Morris and the evil eye.

"All a person needs is faith in the good Lord. Trouble is, sometimes when you believe something, you can make it so."

Grace had been wrong, and she knew it now.

She'd begun to believe Jeremiah was less of a man than others. In so doing, he'd become that in her mind. And she'd started to make him feel that too.

All she had to do was open the drawing pad and see that Jeremiah had his own strengths. This was a man who loved his family and had always tried to do his best for them.

She'd quit pestering him to take them back to the

city, and she'd give him the same love and support in return.

Grace bowed her head and prayed gratitude, filled with wonder and awe at the peace inside her.

27

The lights of the Weyburn ranch
glowed bright as Grady crested the final hill.

He'd have some explaining to do, all right. First of
all, there was the fact that he was late some. Then there
was the fact that he had all the sealed Pony Express
mail pouches but no leather saddlebags to hold the
mail.

It gave Grady pleasure thinking about how the
greenhorn had fooled the outlaw. As Jeremiah had explained when Grady rode up to find him at the fire with
a man too sick to hardly speak, the muddy coat and stolen army horses had said plenty about the visitors.
Turned out Noah did have plenty to be proud of about
his father. Jeremiah had pretended to look for supplies
in the wagon and used that time to take the sealed mail

pouches out of the leather saddlebags and replaced the mail pouches with some sacks of coffee beans. Somewhere out in the storm was a desperado riding hard to escape the law, and all the thief carried was coffee. There was humor in that, Grady figured.

Lastly, Grady had some explaining to do to Lucy Weyburn. That is, after Grady proposed. Then he would tell the woman he loved about her Christmas gift, maybe the best one she'd never receive.

He'd tell Lucy all about how he'd left the cabin and those four boys in renewed heavy snowfall, and how for the next five minutes, all he could see in his mind was how the smile had left that woman's face when she realized Grady had no more gifts. It near broke Grady's heart, thinking of how she must be struggling to raise four boys out here. He remembered how Jeremiah had said he wanted to put a sparkle back in her eyes.

With a long sigh, Grady had turned his horse back to the cabin.

He ignored the barking dog. He stepped off his horse. In his hurry, he didn't shake the new snow off his hat and his shoulders. He was draped in white as he approached the door.

"Ma'am," Grady said, "I'm a little disappointed in myself. I almost rode off without leaving something. It was so small, I forgot it was there."

He had reached into his coat a final time. When he got back to the wagon, he intended to tell Jeremiah about this and take an IOU so that the man could keep his pride and at the same time make his woman happy.

Grady pulled out the gift of Lucy's perfume still wrapped in the fancy silk scarf. Grady set the gift in her hands.

"It's from your husband," Grady said.

Whatever the perfume and scarf had cost Grady, it was worth triple to see the joy on her face.

"Ma'am," Grady said. Lucy was waiting for him at the Weyburn ranch. With or without a gift, he wanted to propose. This was going to be a good Christmas after all. "Merry Christmas and God bless."

He tipped his snowy hat.

As she slowly closed the door, Grady heard the littlest boy speak. "Ma," he asked, "was that man in white an angel?"

"Yes, Caleb," Grady heard her say, "I believe he was."

28

Jeremiah was home now.

Warm and safe in the loft of his cabin.

Grace lay asleep beside him, the sound of her breathing like the music of love. And she'd held him tight falling asleep, tight in a way she hadn't done for months.

Jeremiah wasn't ready to sleep, though. He had plenty to think about this Christmas.

A day had passed. His neighbor had helped him fix the wagon, and Jeremiah had made it home safe with the supplies. That Pony Express man had taken an IOU for Grace's Christmas gift, and by the way Grace had laughed and cried opening it, Jeremiah figured it was the best debt he could have assumed.

Jeremiah had a lot to thank God for.

When that Pony Express rider had first galloped by in

the last light of the afternoon with the storm approaching, even knowing that Noah was losing respect for him, Jeremiah had been so discouraged he couldn't even find the energy to get down from the wagon and build a fire.

In his despair of that moment, he had been willing to admit Grace was right. He was a pitiful man for this wilderness. Couldn't get out of the way of a horse quick enough to save his leg from busting. Couldn't drive a one-horse wagon. Couldn't even fix a broken axle or keep his one horse from running off. Couldn't do enough for his oldest boy to look up to him. There was nothing Jeremiah could do right out here. It was time to pack up all they owned and move back to the city, even if it meant that Jeremiah had squandered his entire inheritance for his dream of a new life in a new land.

Then God had answered Jeremiah's prayer by sending the Pony Express rider back.

But God had given him much more.

The two outlaws had arrived—on his short trip to the wagon to get tea, he'd seen army blankets and army brands on the flanks of the horses—but Jeremiah had not succumbed to fear. He felt some pride that, in deliberately taking so long to find supplies, he'd been cool enough to make sure that Kentucky had ridden off with coffee, not mail, in the Pony Express rider's leather saddlebags. Most of all, in calmly facing death as he expected the bullet from the Winchester, Jeremiah had discovered a strength in himself, and that alone would have been enough of a Christmas gift from God.

But Jeremiah had been given more—a wonder and awe at the workings of the God he trusted. For all of the events that had left Jeremiah stranded in a storm had happened with purpose. So that Jeremiah would be waiting at that fire for a tired and sick man who needed peace. God had wanted to bring back one of his lost loved ones.

Warm and safe in his cabin, Jeremiah thought about another who was now warm and safe.

Reb.

After the Pony Express rider had returned to the wagon and then departed again, Jeremiah had remained at the fire and cradled Reb's head and tried to get him to sip tea.

But Reb had been too far gone to even drink any more of the hot liquid, and all Jeremiah could do was hold the man.

Only a minute earlier, before falling back into his fever, Reb had prayed for Jesus.

When Reb woke again, his eyelids fluttering, Jeremiah had tried to pour some tea into Reb's mouth, but the warm liquid had just dribbled down the man's beard. The man was too far gone.

"Can you hear it?" Reb had asked.

"Hear what?" Jeremiah asked in return. There was only the snapping of embers. Had Kentucky returned?

"Angel music," Reb had said. "All around us. Sweetest sound I ever heard. Ma's singing with them."

Jeremiah had had no chance to reply.

Reb had closed his eyes again and said no more. Reb died quietly, with a smile on his face.